THE FUR P[ERSON]

In hope: *Dear Lady, please*
            Open the door.
            Do not keep me any longer
            Faint from thirst and hunger.

In anger: *May your milk turn sour;*
            May your fish taste queer,
            And your meat look strange,
            From this very hour.

In joy: *I'm a whiffling wonder*
            And my purr's like thunder,
            I'm an elegant fellow
            And my temper's mellow.

       Faithfully translated from
       the original cat by
       MAY SARTON
       in the story of Tom Jones,
           The Fur Person

"People who are successful housekeepers for cats will see how well May Sarton has understood the cat who chose her."
           —*New York Herald Tribune*

SIGNET Titles of Related Interest

The Fur Person

May Sarton

Illustrations by BARBARA KNOX

A SIGNET BOOK from
NEW AMERICAN LIBRARY
TIMES MIRROR

This is an authorized reprint of a hardcover edition published by
W. W. Norton & Company, Inc. The hardcover edition was
published simultaneously in Canada by George J. McLeod
Limited, Toronto.

SIGNET TRADEMARK REG. U.S. PAT. OFF. AND FOREIGN COUNTRIES
REGISTERED TRADEMARK—MARCA REGISTRADA
HECHO EN CHICAGO, U.S.A.

SIGNET BOOKS are published by
The New American Library, Inc.,
1301 Avenue of the Americas, New York, New York 10019

FIRST PRINTING, MARCH, 1970

PRINTED IN THE UNITED STATES OF AMERICA

For Judy

Contents

CHAPTER I

Alexander's Furpiece and the Cat About Town

WHEN he was about two years old, and had been a Cat About Town for some time, glorious in conquests, but rather too thin for comfort, the Fur Person decided that it was time he settled down. This question of finding a permanent home and staff was not one to be approached lightly of a May morning like his casual relationships with various grocers in the neighborhood, kind but vulgar people who did not know how to address a Gentleman Cat. Not at all. This was to be a systematic search for a housekeeper suitable in every way. Every cat knows that the ideal housekeeper is an old maid, if possible living in a small house with a garden. The house should have both an attic and a cellar, the attic for fun and games, the cellar for hunting. Children, I regret to say, are to be avoided whenever possible. They are apt to distract the housekeeper from her duties, and their manners leave much to be desired.

The Fur Person owed his life to a small freckled boy, but he was very good at forgetting things he wished to forget, and this was one of them. It was quite true that the boy named Alexander had howled so loudly when a man from the Animal Rescue League came with a black bag that his mother had relented and said, looking down at the litter, "Well, you may keep just one, Alexander. But you'll have to choose quickly."

"The one with the rather long tail," Alexander said without a moment's hesitation, and dived into the box to rescue the small wobbly velvet pillow who was to turn into the Fur Person, but who was still so small that his ears were not yet unbuttoned and he could barely see out of vague blue eyes. The discomfort of having no mother but only an awkward boy was considerable, but his own proper mother, who would have licked him into shape and provided warm milk whenever he so much as murmured, had disappeared shortly after giving birth to five kittens with very high desperate voices. Instead, Alexander came (when he remembered it) with a medicine dropper and some inferior cow's milk, carried the kitten around inside his leather jacket and was apt to squeeze him rather too tight; that may be why the Fur Person grew into a somewhat long and straggly cat. He slept on Alexander's bed and on very cold nights sometimes wound himself round Alexander's neck, and thus came to be known as Alexander's Furpiece. He bore with Alexander and Alexander's whims until he was nearly six months old. Then one fine summer day, having licked his shirt front into white splendor and examined with pride the white tip of his tail, and seen that every stripe was glossy along his tiger back, he swaggered out like any young dandy, and what began as an extended rove and ramble ended in a way of life, for he never came back.

As a Cat About Town he developed a stiff hippy walk; he had a very small nick taken out of one ear; and sometimes he was too busy to bother about washing for days at a time. His shirt front became gray, the white tip of his tail almost disappeared, and his whiskers sprang out from his cheeks with the strength and vitality of porcupine quills. He learned a great variety of street songs, how to terrify without lifting a paw, how to wail a coward into retreat, how to scream a bully into attacking just a fraction of a second too soon, how to court a gentle middle-aged tabby as well as many a saucy young thing; he was kept extremely busy right on into the fall, and, I am afraid, he forgot all about Alexander. His expeditions and conquests took him far afield and when he did, at an off moment, remember the soft bed of his kittenhood he was not quite sure where to find it again. I am myself, he thought, lashing his tail back and forth, a formidable, an irresistible Cat About Town, and that is enough to be. It was a full-time job. The question of

food, for instance, continually in-
terrupted other and more interesting
pursuits. A Cat About Town must be
wily as well as ferocious, must know
every inch of a territory for the wob-
bliest garbagecan lids, must learn the
time when local grocers are apt to fling
a few tasty haddock heads and tails to
anyone who may be about just then; he
must learn how to persuade old ladies
into handing out bowls of milk, or even
an occasional saucer of cream, without ever allowing himself to be cap-
tured, must in fact hunt out kindness
with ruthless self-interest, but never
give in to any such dreams of comfort
as might involve a loss of Independence. It is an arduous life and the Cat
About Town is a lean mocking charac-
ter for whom human beings are to be
used for what they are worth, which is
not much.

The Fur Person, at this time of his
life, was no exception; he conformed
to type, except when he was curled up
into a tight ball under a hedge and
sometimes made a small whirring noise
which resembled a purr, and sometimes
even opened his paws and closed them
again as if he were remembering some-

thing delicious, but when he woke up he had always forgotten what it was. Only once in a while he felt rather wistful and gave his face and shirt front a lick to cheer himself up, and swaggered down the street a fraction more aggressively than usual, and then stopped, looked back, seemed for a moment not to know where he was, or even perhaps who he was.

By the time he was two years old, he was still a Cat About Town, but he was a Cat About Town who had strange dreams, dreams of an open fire and himself with his paws tucked in sitting in front of it, of a gentle hand quite unlike a small boy's hand, of a saucer of warm milk—very strange dreams indeed. They required concentrated yoga exercises to forget, and sometimes he was haunted by one for as much as a whole day.

And one morning when he woke up purring from his dream, he washed his face very carefully and decided that it was time he settled down. His whiskers shone in the sun. He stretched, yawned, and then amused himself for a few moments by scaring the pigeons waddling under an elm a few yards

away. But in the middle of this childish game, he suddenly sat quite upright, narrowed his eyes, then opened
them very wide and looked at nothing
for a long time. It was here at this very
spot that he realized that he was an
orphan. His face grew quite pointed
with self-pity and it was all he could
do to maintain his dignity and not utter
the long wail of loneliness which he
felt rising within him.

This experience was followed by a
hard day, a day of aimless wandering
and of painful encounters with fat
sleek cats sitting on porches, whom he
now regarded in an entirely new
light; they had found housekeepers;
they had snug warm beds. By the time
dark was falling, the Fur Person was
very tired, walking down a strange
street alone, and he knew in his bones
that the time for decision was at hand.

Then he heard a gentle human voice
calling, "Here kitty, kitty, kitty," from
somewhere quite far away. Even a
week ago this sound would not have
concerned him at all. But now in an instant he was alert and trotted amiably
along to reconnoiter. He could see a
stout woman with gray hair stand-

ing in the lighted doorway of a house, all surrounded by a garden. There was no little boy in sight, and the Fur Person felt strongly drawn to the place. He ran around a barberry bush and sat down where he could observe matters, and he was about to make up his mind, when a very peculiar-looking cat suddenly raced up the steps and disappeared inside as the door closed. The cat was beige colored with dark brown paws and ears and—was the Fur Person in a slightly hallucinated state?—seemed to have blue eyes like a human being.

It was a moment of bitterness even to a nature as philosophical, as used to Hard Knocks as the Fur Person. Another cat was already in possession! Another cat was lord of the garden, the little pear tree, the beautifully soft earth in the flower beds (just right for certain purposes), and above all of the kindly old woman with the gentle voice. He had found this perfect haven too late.

The Fur Person raced up the pear tree just to give himself confidence, and then raced down again, without even stopping to sharpen his claws. On

an impulse he ran to the back door, for
there were lights in what must be the
kitchen. Then gently and politely he
scratched a little at the screen door.
There was no response. He began to
miss Alexander. He even thought without distaste of the boring food from a
can with a stupid-looking cat face on
it, which was all Alexander ever fed
him. He was, in fact, ravenously hungry
and exhausted. He scratched a little
again and gave a very polite mew, a
restrained   mew,   considering   the
violence of his feelings, considering
that only a day before he had been a
wild and wily Cat About Town. He
imagined the peculiar cat lifting a paw
toward some delicious lamb or beef
liver being cut up at this very moment
by the kind old lady into convenient
small pieces and lightly sautéed in bacon fat. It was really too much, and
now suddenly under the full force of
emotion he found himself singing an
entirely new song, a song he made up
himself. It went something like this:

> Dear Lady, please
> Open the door.
> Do not keep me any longer

Faint from thirst and hunger
But have pity
On an orphan kitty,
Hear my mews!

It was not too bad a song, he felt, for
a first try and when it was finished, because he was a Gentleman Cat, he
turned his back and sat down, as if perfectly indifferent, though his heart was
beating very fast, and one ear could
not be persuaded to stay pointed forward, but turned backward, rather in-
elegantly, to listen. Sure enough, the
door opened.

"Well," said a not very pleased voice,
"where did you come from? Hungry,
are you?"

The Fur Person, according to the
First Commandment of the Gentleman
Cat ("When addressed, do not move a
muscle. Look as if you hadn't heard.")
just gazed soulfully in the opposite di-
rection.

"You'd better go home now," the
voice said, not unkindly. Unfortunately
at this moment a cloud of scent, the
scent of fresh cod boiling on the stove,
came and settled around the Fur Person like a nimbus. He was after all,

still a young cat, and at this instant
karma was stronger than any rule or
regulation. He really did not know how
it happened, but the next thing he did
know was that he was in the kitchen,
spirited there as Odysseus into the
arms of Circe by the ineffable cod
(sacred, as you all know, and hence
having perhaps some attributes of a
mystical kind). He was also, unfortunately, spirited into the furious pres-
ence of the peculiar cat, who sprang
at him and succeeded in scratching
him on the small cinnamon square of
his nose in the tenderest place. This
was no time for poetry; the Fur Person
gave a scream of outrage and shot out
into the night. "Hear my mews" indeed, he said to himself, growling. And
he went on his way shouting in a very
piercing voice, so the whole neighborhood was alarmed:

> May your milk turn sour;
> May your fish taste queer,
> And your meat look strange,
> From this very hour;
> May your blue eyes blear;
> May you get the mange.

It was such a good curse that he repeated it, making a few changes in the inflection, just to try it out. He was so pleased with it that he forgot to be hungry and lonely any more and curled up in some delicious wood shavings in a basket outside the grocery store, and slept the sleep of satisfied anger.

CHAPTER II

An Adventure

EARLY in the morning he was still curled up into a ball, one paw clasping his nose, so he was perfectly airtight and warm, when he was roused from a delicious dream about some affectionate and playful mice by an infernal noise, a noise so tremendous that it sounded as if several houses were collapsing, and all the china and saucepans in them being hurled violently about by a giant. The Fur Person sprang up without even opening his eyes and vanished behind the grocery store. When he was able to open his eyes—they seemed to be glued together—he crept back to see if there was anything left of the world, but just then there was another huge crash and bang. Luckily this time his eyes were open and he saw that this earthquake was merely the ashman emptying the barrels. So, like any Gentleman Cat who has just been badly scared (Second Commandment: "When frightened, look bored."), he sat very erect and still and did some yoga exercises to calm himself down. This meant sitting with his paws tucked in and forcing himself to think of nothing at all; it is quite hard to do.

What with the events of the night before and the fact that his bed had now disappeared into the ashman's truck and was on its way to the town dump, what with the cold gray morning light and the thought of that horrible blue-eyed cat having a sumptuous breakfast no doubt at this very moment, the Fur Person felt very depressed. He lifted one paw in hesitation, looked at it thoughtfully and then became absorbed in washing it, so that all decisions were put off for the time being. For the first thing a Gentleman Cat does in the morning is to be sure that his suit is thoroughly pressed and damped, and his shirt front immaculate. While busy with this absorbing job, he considered himself with an impersonal and thoughtful eye. Perhaps he was rather too thin and his tail a trifle long, but after all, he reminded himself, it does have a small white tip. That is quite a distinction. And no one could deny that a white shirt front and white paws went very well with a glossy tiger coat and set off the wide black bands looped across his breast, rather like a Lord Mayor of London's chains. He told himself that he was not the handsomest cat in town, but reasonably distinguished as cats of his family went, and he gave his whiskers a good deal more than a lick and a promise. In fact his right front paw had been moistened and rubbed his face at least fifty times that morning, and his tongue was quite tired.

He had just stopped to rest, giving a long stretch first of his front legs then of his back, so that he looked longer than ever, when the grocer drew up in a big black car, got out, swinging his keys in a rather cheerful way, and began to open the various locks on the door of

his shop. The Fur Person instantly
thought of milk, even a small piece of
cheese perhaps, or some hamburger,
and explained his plight to the grocer
by rubbing against the doorjamb and
then slipping in, his tail straight up in
the air like a flag, and every bit of his
person saying, "Thank you very much,
nice morning, isn't it?"

"I haven't seen you before, have I?"
said the grocer. "Hungry?"

It was delicious to feel the low thun-
der of purrs rumbling inside him. Dur-
ing his years of being a Cat About
Town he had only purred in his sleep,
but now he began to roar with pleasure
like a little stove. He could feel every
hair of his fur coat trembling with the
force of these purrs; he swayed slightly
as he sat down, lifting his head in pure
hope to the grocer's face. Of course the
grocer, a simple fat man of no graces,
could hardly appreciate the refinement
of ecstasy which he was witnessing.
But he did seem to get the crude point
even if he did not appreciate its nu-
ances. In a very few moments, he had
poured out some milk in a saucer and
laid beside it on a piece of newspaper
some hamburger, of uncertain age. The

Fur Person approached the milk, breathed above it for a few seconds, and then actually settled down, wrapping his tail around him, his two front paws close together. When the saucer was empty he moved over to the hamburger with eager anticipation. Alas, it was not worthy of a Gentleman Cat, and though he was still very hungry, he rose up with immense dignity and scratched at the newspaper as if to cover up this unfortunate meal, that it never be seen again.

"Not as hungry as you look, eh?" said the grocer cruelly. The Fur Person gave him a long indignant look, his green eyes as wide open as they could be, then slowly shut them on the vulgarity of the grocer. Still, it was not to be supposed that he would find the perfectly suitable establishment on the very first day of his search, and, all things considered, the grocer's shop might be as good a base camp as he could find. So the Fur Person assumed his usual habits; as it was now time to read the newspaper, he jumped up into the big window and settled down comfortably, his paws tucked in, to see what was going on in the world. Clever cats know that this time in the morning is dogtime and generally sit indoors looking out. It is very thrilling to learn the news in this way. The Fur Person opened his eyes wide when a St. Bernard sauntered past, and then a poodle went by like lightning. But when Hannah came into sight, he was quite beside himself with excitement and pressed his nose to the pane, for Hannah lived on Alexander's street. Every morning she ran the whole length of the street announcing the morning news in a series of loud excited barks and thus she was known as "the barky dog." She was a beagle and very much too fat, the Fur Person thought; being so thin himself, the fat of others disgusted him. It lacked elegance. He was amazed to see Hannah so far from home. Whatever could she be doing? She stood by the window and seemed to recognize him, for she became very barky indeed. The Fur Person, offended by so much noise, withdrew and turned his back on her. The only sign that he was paying attention was a slight raising of the fur along his spine (he could not prevent this though Hannah was beneath such notice, noisy gossip that she was). His long thin tail had suddenly become enormous.

He had been so busy not listening to Hannah and pretending not to mind her voice that he had not noticed the arrival of a customer.

"Good morning, Mrs. Seaver, you're an early bird," said the grocer in the falsely jovial tone that grocers often employ. It was a tone the Fur Person recognized at once, the tone people used who said "Nice Kitty" but really did not like cats.

"I ran out of coffee," said Mrs. Seaver, helping herself to a bag on the shelf. "Want to grind this for me, percolator—" but she had hardly finished this sentence when she saw the Fur Person, glorious, every hair shining in the sun, his tail beautifully enlarged by his anger at Hannah, his green eyes observing her with obvious interest. "Ooooooh," she crooned, "you have a lovely kitty. Where did you come from, Kitty?" she asked in a foolish tone of voice, as if he were feebleminded or only a few weeks old. But she leaned over and scratched him under his chin and no Gentleman Cat can resist such an attention. He got up, arched his back and thanked her kindly.

"He was out there, waiting at the door, like he belonged here," said the grocer. "Not even hungry," he lied without so much as batting an eyelash.

The customer was stroking the Fur Person down his arched back now, in a way very consoling to an orphan. "Mmmm" she murmured in his ear as if she were contemplating a lobster dinner, "I do love cats." The Fur Person should have been warned by something cannibalistic in this tone, but it must be remembered that he was young and inexperienced in the ways of human love, and besides he was very hungry. The ecstasy began to thrum inside him again and before he knew it, he was purring away, and even lifting one paw into the air and spreading out the claws, out and in, out and in, from sheer pleasure.

"Will you look at that? Isn't he the cutest thing?" the lady crooned. "You wouldn't let me have him, would you?" she asked the grocer.

"He ain't mine to give. Take him along if you like him."

The Fur Person had no time to consider this proposition or to get a word in edgewise. Before he knew what had happened, he was lifted up into the air and hanging down awkwardly over the lady's arm. He struggled, but she put a hand over his nose and said, "Oh no, you don't." Very well, he thought, wait and see. Maybe she had a little house with an attic and a cellar and garden with neat beds of flowers and good earth, and maybe she had lobster every day for lunch. He kept very quiet, but his eyes were enormous with expectation, and his long tail hanging down under her arm, twitched back and forth with excitement.

He leaned way out to see where they were going. His ears pricked as they approached a dear little house and a garden, but they passed it by. He was rather disconcerted, and made a half-hearted attempt to jump down when the Lady turned in before a huge brick apartment house. By now it was too late. He looked up into the Lady's soft foolish face with alarm, for she had suddenly become a jailer. But he really did need some breakfast, and after breakfast he would try to make a discreet withdrawal. So he told himself, as she finally set him down in a tiny dark hall.

CHAPTER III

An Escape

THE Fur Person raised his head and took in a terrible series of smells, the smell of a small stuffy apartment, of overheated radiators, of cheap perfume, of talcum powder, of yesterday's bacon; he stood there, his tail standing out straight behind him in amazement, his nose trembling slightly in dismay. Then he cast a quick glance behind him, but the door was shut tight. No escape. The lady meanwhile had not stopped talking since she set him down. He could hear her while she ran water in the kitchen and rattled the dishes, telling him over and over (almost as

bad as Hannah she was) how much she
loved kitties, how much she loved him,
and what he would have for breakfast.
The Fur Person could not pay attention right away to this. He had first to
explore the apartment and any possible
avenues of escape. He had first to sniff
at every inch of the dirty pink carpet
stretched from wall to wall, with moldy
crumbs, as he soon discovered, concealed along the edges. He had never
been in a human house with so many
objects in it, and he was only about a
third of the way through, had in fact
just reached a stand with three potted
ferns on it, had stood up on his hindlegs
to feel the quality of a green velvet armchair (for claw-sharpening purposes),
had taken a quick look at the bed, almost entirely covered with small satin
pillows and with, of all things, an imita-
tion cat sitting on it, when the lady
suddenly pounced on him from the
back and hauled him ignominiously into the kitchen, setting him down in
front of a plate of scrambled eggs and
bacon. Now, no Gentleman Cat likes to
be plunked down in front of his food.
The law is that he shall approach it
slowly from a distance, without haste,

however hungry he may be, that he shall smell it from afar and decide at least three feet away what his verdict is going to be: Good, Fair, Passable or Unworthy.

If the verdict is Good, he will approach it very slowly, settle himself down in a crouching position and curl his tail around him before he takes a mouthful. If it is Fair, he will crouch, but leave his tail behind him, stretched out along the floor. If it is merely Passable, he will eat standing up, and if it is Unworthy he will perform the rite of pretending to scratch earth over it and bury it.

The Fur Person backed away, ruffled and indignant, and had to put his clothes in order before he would even look at the food. Then he very carefully extracted the bacon, bit by bit, and ate it with considerable relish. Scrambled eggs were considered "Unworthy" and were left on the plate.

When the lady saw him performing the usual rite demanded by Unworthy food, she clapped her hands with delight and said he was a terribly clever cat (little she knew!), she had never seen anything so sweet in her life, and he should have a can of crabmeat for his lunch.

Then she picked him up and tried to fold him together onto her lap. Foolish woman! Though a little crumbled bacon is not a heavy meal for a Gentleman Cat who has spent the night out, it is enough of a meal to require at least fifteen minutes of solitary meditation after it. The Fur Person jumped down at once and went as far away from her as he could get, as her smell of cheap narcissus or rose (he was not quite sure which) made him feel rather ill. The farthest away he could get was under the bed; there he stayed for some time, licking his chops, for the slightest sensation of oiliness or fat around his whiskers is something a Gentleman Cat cannot endure. Then he sat, crouching, but not in any way "settled" and thought things over. He did not fancy the lady, but she had mentioned crabmeat for lunch. Also there was at present no way of escape that he could see. By now, it should be clear that the Fur Person was of a philosophical nature, capable of considerable reflection. He had waited six months before making up his mind to leave Alexander and

two years before deciding to settle
down, and after all, he had only been
here for half an hour. Sometimes first
impressions could be misleading. Also
he was very susceptible to flattery, and
the lady's admiration was unstinted.
Although he was completely concealed
from her under the bed, she was still
talking about him and to him. Things
could be worse.

The trouble was, as he soon found
out, that as soon as he came into reach,
the lady could not resist hugging and
kissing him with utter disregard for the
dignity of his person. There are times
when a Gentleman Cat likes very much
to be scratched gently under his chin,
and if this is done with *savoir-faire* he
may afterwards enjoy a short siesta on
a lap and some very refined stroking,
but he does not like to be held upside
down like a human baby and he does
not like to be cooed over, and to be
pressed to a bosom smelling of narcissus
or rose. The Fur Person struggled furiously against the ardent ministrations
of the lady and took refuge behind the
garbage pail in the kitchen when he
could. It was crystal clear that he was
in jail, and, even at the risk of not hav-

ing crabmeat for lunch, he must escape.
His eyes behind the garbage pail had
become slits; he did not tuck his paws
in but sat upright, thinking very fast.
While he was thinking he nibbled one
back foot—he had observed before that
there was nothing like thinking to make
one itch all over—then he had to bite a
place rather difficult to reach on his
back, and then his front paw, and soon
he was quite absorbed in licking himself all over. It is best to be clean before
attempting   to   escape,   and—this
thought occurred to him suddenly—it
is also best to have sharp claws. From
behind the garbage pail he could see
the green velvet armchair, and as soon
as the lady disappeared for a moment
into the bedroom, he emerged from
his hiding place and stretched, then
walked sedately to the chair, sat up and
began to sharpen his claws on the thick
plush, a very satisfactory claw-sharpening place indeed.

"Oh," screamed the lady, and
swooped down and picked him up,
"you naughty cat. Stop it at once!" She
even shook him quite violently. This, on
top of all he had suffered that morning,
was suddenly more than the Fur Per-

son could endure. He turned and bit
her arm, not very hard, but just enough
so she dropped him unceremoniously
and gave a penetrating yell.

"You're not a nice cat at all," she
said, and she began to whimper. "You
don't like me," she whimpered, "do
you?"

But this last remark was addressed to
his back. He was sitting in front of the
door. It is a known fact that if one sits
long enough in front of a door, doing
the proper yoga exercises, the door will
open. It is not necessary to indulge in
childish noises. Commandment Four:
"A Gentleman Cat does not mew except
in extremity. He makes his wishes
known and then waits." So he sat with
his back to the lady and wished with
the whole force of his fur person; his
whiskers even trembled slightly with
the degree of concentration. Meanwhile
the lady grumbled and mumbled to
herself and said "Nobody loves me."
But the Fur Person's whiskers only
trembled a little more violently, so huge
had become his wish to get away. By
comparison with this prison, the grocery shop looked like Heaven. He might
even bring himself to eat day-old ham-

burger if only he could get away from this infernal apartment. He noticed also that it was much too hot and his skin was prickling all over, but he schooled himself not to move, not to lick, not to nibble. He became a single ever-more-powerful WISH TO GET OUT.

"Very well," said the lady, blowing her nose. He gave her one last cold look out of his green eyes, and then she opened the door. She even followed him downstairs, his tail held perfectly straight like a flag to show his thanks, and opened the front door. The Fur Person bounded out and ran all the way up the street, sniffing the fresh air with intense pleasure. He ran halfway up an elm tree and down again before you could say "Gentleman Cat," and then he sauntered down the street, his tail at half-mast, and his heart at peace.

CHAPTER IV

A Dish of Haddock

ON HIS roves and rambles, on his rounds and travels, he had never found himself exactly where he now found himself, on the border of a dangerous street—very dangerous, he realized after a short exposure to the roar of cars, the squeaking of brakes, the lurching, weaving, rumbling, interspersed with loud bangs and horns of a really incredible amount of traffic. It was quite bewildering, and the Fur Person looked about for a place where he could withdraw and sit awhile. He was rather tired. It was time, he considered, for a short snooze, after which the ques-

tion of Lunch might be approached in
the proper frame of mind. And there,
providentially indeed, he noticed that
he was standing in front of a house
bounded on one side by a porch with a
very suitable railing running along it.
He took the porch in one leap, sat for a
second measuring the distance to the
square platform on top of the railing
post, then swung up to it rather casu-
ally, and there he was, safe and free as
you please, in a little patch of sunlight
which seemed to have been laid down
there just for him. He tucked in his
paws and closed his eyes. The sun was
delicious on his back, so much so that
he began to sing very softly, accompanying himself this time with one of his
lighter purrs, just a tremolo to keep
things going.

And there he sat for maybe an hour,
or maybe even two, enjoying the peace
and quiet, and restoring himself after
the rather helter-skelter life he had
been leading for two days, since his
metamorphosis into a Gentleman Cat
in search of a housekeeper. He was so
deep down in the peace and the quiet
that when a window went up right beside him on the porch, he did not jump

into the air as he might have done had
it not been such a very fine May morning or had he been a little less tired.
As it was, he merely opened his eyes
very wide and looked.

"Come here," a voice said inside the
house, "there's a pussin on the porch."

The Fur Person waited politely, for
he had rather enjoyed the timbre of
the voice, quite low and sweet, and he
was always prepared to be admired.
Pretty soon two faces appeared in the
window and looked at him, and he
looked back.

"Well," said another voice, "perhaps
he would like some lunch."

The Fur Person woke right up then,
rose, and stretched on the tips of his
toes, his tail making a wide arc to keep
his balance.

"He is rather thin," said the first
voice. "I wonder where he belongs.
We've never seen him before, have we?"

"And what are we having for
lunch?" said the second voice.

"There's that haddock left over—I
could cream it."

The Fur Person pivoted on the fence
post and stamped three times with his

back feet, to show how dearly he loved the sound of haddock.

"What is he doing now?" said the first voice and chuckled.

"Saying he likes haddock, I expect."

Then, quite unexpectedly, the window was closed. Dear me, he thought, won't I do? For the first time, he began to be really anxious about his appearance. Was the tip of his tail as white as it could be? How about his shirt front? Dear me, he thought, won't I do? And his heart began to beat rather fast, for he was, after all, tired and empty and in a highly emotional state. This made him unusually impulsive. He jumped down to the porch and then to the ground below and trotted round to the back door, for as he expected, there was a garden at the back, with a pear tree at the end of it, and excellent posts for claw-sharpening in a small laundry yard. He could not resist casting a glance at the flower beds, nicely dug up and raked, in just the right condition for making holes, and in fact the thought of a neat little hole was quite irresistible, so he dug one there and then.

When he had finished, he saw that

the crocuses were teeming with bees.
His whiskers trembled. He crouched
down in an ecstasy of impatience and
coiled himself tight as a spring, lashed
his tail, and before he knew it himself
was in the air and down like lightning
on an unsuspecting crocus. The bee
escaped, though the crocus did not.
Well, thought the Fur Person, a little
madness in the spring is all very well,
but I must remember that this is serious business and I must get down to it.
So he sat and looked the house over. It
was already evident that there were in-
numerable entrances and exits like the
window opening to the porch, that
there were places of safety in case he
was locked out, and that (extraordinary bit of luck) he had found not one
old maid with a garden and a house but
two. Still, his hopes had been dashed
rather often in the last twenty-four
hours and he reminded himself this
time to be circumspect and hummed a
bit of the tune about being a free cat,
just to give himself courage.

Then he walked very slowly, stopping to stretch out one back leg and
lick it, for he remembered the Fifth
Commandment: "Never hurry towards

an objective, never look as if you had only one thing in mind, it is not polite." Just as he was nibbling the muscle in his back foot with considerable pleasure, for he was always discovering delightful things about himself, he heard the back door open. Cagey, now, he told himself. So he went on nibbling and even spread his toes and licked his foot quite thoroughly, and all this time, a very sweet voice was saying:

"Are you hungry, puss-cat? Come, pussin..."

And so at last he came, his tail tentatively raised in a question mark; he came slowly, picking up his paws with care, and gazing all the while in a quite romantic way (for he couldn't help it) at the saucer held in the old maid's hand. At the foot of the back stairs he sat down and waited the necessary interval.

"Well, come on," said the voice, a slightly impatient one, with a little roughness to it, a great relief after the syrupy lady in the hot apartment from which he had escaped.

At this the Fur Person bounded up the stairs, and at the very instant he

entered the kitchen, the purrs began to
swell inside him and he wound himself
round and round two pairs of legs (for
he must be impartial), his nose in the
air, his tail straight up like a flag, on
tiptoe, and roaring with thanks.

"He's awfully thin," said the first
voice.

"And not very beautiful, I must
say," said the second voice.

But the Fur Person fortunately was
not listening. He was delicately and
with great deliberation sniffing the
plate of haddock; he was settling down;
he was even winding his tail around
him, because here at last was a meal
worthy of a Gentleman Cat.

CHAPTER V

A Home-coming

THE most remarkable thing about
the two kind ladies was that they left
him to eat in peace and did not say one
word. They had the tact to withdraw
into the next room and to talk about
other things, and leave him entirely to
himself. It seemed to him that he had
been looked up and down, remarked
upon, and hugged and squeezed far too
much in the last days, and now he was
terribly grateful for the chance to savor
this delicious meal with no exclaiming
this or that, and without the slightest
interruption. When he had finished
every single scrap and then licked over

the plate several times (For if a meal is Worthy, the Sixth Commandment says, "The plate must be left clean, so clean that a person might think it had been washed."), the Fur Person sat up and licked his chops. He licked them perhaps twenty or twenty-five times, maybe even fifty times, his raspberry-colored tongue devoting itself to each whisker, until his face was quite clean. Then he began on his front paws and rubbed his face gently with a nice wet piece of fur, and rubbed right over his ears, and all this took a considerable time. While he was doing it he could hear a steady gentle murmur of conversation in the next room and pretty soon he stopped with one paw in the air, shook it once, shook his head the way a person does whose hair has just been washed in the bowl, and then took a discreet ramble.

"Just make yourself at home," said the voice he liked best. "Just look around."

His tail went straight up so they would understand that he was out for a rove and did not intend, at the moment, to catch a mouse, that in fact he was looking around, and not commit-

ting himself one way or another. The
house, he discovered, was quite large
enough, quite nice and dark, with a
long hall for playing and at least three
sleeping places. He preferred a bed, but
there was a large comfortable armchair
that would do in a pinch. Still, he reminded himself, one must not be hasty.
Just then he walked into a rather small
room lined with books and with (this
was really splendid) a huge flat desk
in it. There are times in a Gentleman
Cat's life when what he likes best is to
stretch out full length (and the Fur
Person's length was considerable) on a
clean hard place. The floor is apt to be
dirty and to smell of old crumbs, but a
desk, preferably with papers strewn
across it, is quite the thing. The Fur
Person felt a light elegant obbligato of
purrs rising in his throat.

Neither of the old maids had, until
now, touched him. And this, he felt,
was a sign of understanding. They had
given him a superior lunch and allowed
him to rove and ramble in peace. Now
he suddenly felt quite curious to discover what they were like. It is amazing
how much a cat learns about life by the
way he is stroked. His heart was beat-

ing rather fast as he approached the
table. One of the two old maids had
almost disappeared in a cloud of smoke,
the brusque one; he did not like smoke,
so he made a beeline toward the other,
gazing out of wide-open eyes, preceded
by his purrs.

"Well, old thing, do you want a lap?"
the gentle voice inquired very politely.
She did not reach down and gather him
up. She leaned forward and ran one
finger down his head and along his
spine. Then she scratched him between
the ears in a most delightful way. The
purrs began to sound like bass drums
very lightly drummed, and the Fur
Person felt himself swell with pleasure.
It was incredibly enjoyable, after all he
had been through, to be handled with
such *savoir-faire*, and before he knew
it himself he had jumped up on this
welcoming lap and begun to knead.
The Fur Person, you remember, had
lost his mother when he was such a
small kitten that his ears were still but-
toned down and his eyes quite blue,
but when he jumped up onto this lady's
lap, he seemed dimly to remember
kneading his mother like this, with tiny

starfish paws that went in and out, in and out.

"I wish he'd settle," the gentle voice said, "his claws are rather sharp."

But the Fur Person did not hear this for he was in a trance of home-coming and while he kneaded he composed a song, and while he composed it, it seemed as if every hair on his body tingled and was burnished, so happy was he at last.

"He actually looks fatter," the brusque voice said, "he must have been awfully hungry."

The Fur Person closed his eyes and sang his song and it went like this:

> Thank you, thank you,
> You and no other
> Dear gentle voice,
> Dear human mother,
> For your delicate air,
> For your *savoir-faire*
> For your kind soft touch
> Thank you very much.

He was so terribly sleepy that the last line became inextricably confused in a purr and in his suddenly making himself into a round circle of peace, all kneading spent, and one paw over his nose.

There was an indefinite interval of silence; but it must not be forgotten that the Fur Person had led a hectic and disillusioning life, and while he slept his nose twitched and his paws twitched and he imagined that he was caught and being smothered, and before he even quite woke up or had his eyes open he had leapt off the kind lap, in a great state of nerves.

It is all very well, he told himself severely, but this time you have to be careful. Remember Alexander, remember the grocer, remember the lady and her suffocating apartment. It was not easy to do, but without giving the old maids a parting look, he walked in great dignity down the long dark hall to the front door and sat down before it, wishing it to open. Pretty soon he heard footsteps, but he did not turn his head. I must have time to think this over, he was telling himself. Never be hasty when choosing a housekeeper. The door opened and he was outside. Never be hasty, he was telling himself, as he bounded down the steps and into the sweet May afternoon. But at the same time, quite without intending it, he found that he had composed a short poem, and as he sharpened his claws on the elm by the door and as he ran up it, just to show what a fine Gentleman Cat he was, he hummed it over. It was very short and sweet:

East and West
Home is best.

And though he spent several days coming and going, it was very queer how, wherever he went, he always found himself somehow coming back to the two old maids, just to be sure they were still there, and also, it must be confessed, to find out what they were having for supper. And on the fourth day it rained and that settled it: he spent the night. The next morning while he was washing his face after eating a nice little dish of stew beef cut up into small pieces, he made his decision. After all, if a Gentleman Cat spends the night, it is a kind of promise. I will be your cat, he said to himself, sitting on the desk with his paws tucked in and his eyes looking gravely at the two old maids standing in the doorway, if you

will be my housekeepers. And of course
they agreed, because of the white tip to
his tail, because he hummed such a
variety of purrs and songs, because he
really was quite a handsome fellow,
and because they had very soft hearts.

CHAPTER VI

The Fur Person Gets a Name and Fights a Nameless Cat

UNTIL he had made up his mind where he was going to live and with whom, the Fur Person, although he minded being an orphan, had not ever stopped to think that he had no name. It was all very well to think of himself as a Cat About Town, or Gentleman Cat, but after all there were other Cats About Town, and a great many Gentlemen Cats in the neighborhood, so he was delighted when he heard the gentle-voiced housekeeper say, just as she was pouring her third cup of tea, "I think we should call him Tom Jones—

after all, he was a foundling—and so was Henry Fielding's Tom Jones."

"Plain, but distinguished and notable in the history of English letters," Brusque Voice answered, stooping down to give him a small piece of buttered scone which he enjoyed very much.

His name seemed to give his housekeepers almost as much satisfaction as it gave him, and after that he always managed to be present whenever guests came to the house so that he could have the pleasure of being formally introduced. Once, when he had decided to reward Gentle Voice for a particularly good breakfast by accompanying her to the corner, he was delighted to hear a neighbor inquire, "And how is Mr. Jones this morning?"

He walked back from the corner so aglow with self-respect that he did not notice that he was being sneered at by a nameless gray cat behind the snowball bush, that in fact the nameless cat was out for revenge, that he had registered Tom Jones's sleek appearance and obvious narcissism and was going to take him down a peg.

"Think you're somebody, do you?" sneered the nameless cat.

Tom Jones stopped where he was and took in the situation. The snowball bush was just beside the porch. Well, it is beneath my notice to answer this sort of gutter talk. I'll just go the long way round, he thought, pretend that I didn't hear that rude remark—pure jealousy of course and best ignored. Under these circumstances a Gentleman Cat's walk becomes a thing of poise and art. His legs seem a bit stiffer than usual and he walks with extreme gravity and slowness. It takes courage to do this, to ignore an insult from a nameless cat who is prepared to throw dignity to the wind, and pounce. But Mr. Jones of course did not need lessons in deportment. The slowness, the primness, the self-sufficiency of his walk would have silenced any ordinary nameless cat. This one, however, was mad with love for the tortoise shell next door, called Nelly. And in his madness he paid not the slightest attention to being ignored. In fact he rose up, swelled to huge proportions by rage, and stalked after Tom Jones, rank pride stiffening his legs so that he looked as if

he were a giant on stilts. Tom Jones felt
this, but he did not of course deign to
look back. He walked on down the
path, only stopping once to nibble his
leg, just to show how perfectly indifferent he was.

"Oh no, you don't," said the nameless cat, and began to sing a rude song.
He sang it at a high pitch so that it
came out piercingly, a very intense
song indeed. Tom Jones, who had re-
spect for poetic invention even when
used against himself, turned right
round, and crouched down, his eyes
thin slits of attention.

> You're thin and lanky,
> You're underbred;
> Though you may feel swanky,
> You've a common head.
> Hoity-toity, frowsy-browsy,
> You've been spoiled rotten,
> Your fur is lousy.
> No one has forgotten,
> Though you have a name
> You're an orphan cat
> And a gutter bum
> For all of that.
> So here I come,

And look out, Jones,
For I'll break your bones!

Of course there was no question of the nameless cat's actually coming for a long while yet. This would have been a sign of weakness. He and the Fur Person crouched down and settled in with about four feet between them while the insults flew all about and around them. The first song was really just the tuning up. Tom Jones listened to it in complete silence, partly because he was busy preparing an answer, and it would never do to run dry at such a moment. However, the words "gutter bum" sent a shiver of rage through his whiskers, and he gave a low growl. Otherwise he was perfectly motionless. Then slowly and in quite a gentle voice he made his answer with withering scorn.

You're wasting your time
With that clumsy rhyme
And your pompous verse
Just couldn't be worse
For it's terribly clear
That you're jealous, my dear.

Why not wash your face
(It's a public disgrace)
And leave poetry
To the likes of me
And the breaking of bones
To Terrible Jones.

The last two lines of this verse were made effective by the fact that the whole first part was sung in a minor key, in a sneering tone, but at the very end on "Terrible Jones" the Fur Person achieved a piercing and terrible scream, which made the hackles rise on his own back and produced a quite extraordinary effect on the enemy. For the nameless gray cat now slithered forward, his stomach close to the ground, making himself as long as possible until his bright pink nose was only one inch from Tom Jones's cinnamon nose. Just here, with terrifying self-control, he stopped dead and glared his answer. Confronted with this bristling angry face, with two torn ears above it and the look of furious contempt which leapt out of the gray cat's eyes like lightning, Tom Jones was suddenly aware that he had got himself into a real fight. There

was no way of backing down now, and
he began his serious moan (rather like
bagpipes played by a Scottish Regi-
ment as it goes into battle), which is
the sign that the time for words is rap-
idly drawing to a close. The gray cat
accompanied this moan with his own
version of it and then whiffled once.
The whiffle was a warning: Tom Jones
sprang right up into the air just as the
gray cat pounced so they actually
bumped into each other and came
down screaming with rage, biting whatever seemed handy. The gray cat got
hold of Tom Jones's lower lip, and hung
on. All this time they were both hurling
insults at each other and the concate-
nation of screams, growls and yells of
pain (for Tom Jones's lip was spurting
blood now and he had a bad scratch on
his tender nose while the gray cat felt
a whole patch of fur being torn out of
his neck) was dreadful to hear. It was
quite impossible to tell who was win-
ning at this point, and no one will ever
know, for just then Brusque Voice came
out on the porch and threw a whole
pail of water at them, and added her
voice to Tom Jones's, shouting, "Go
away, you horrible cat!" The gray cat

had received most of the water right in his face and he flew off down the street, still growling and cursing all housekeepers and Gentlemen Cats who could rely on such unfair methods to win a fight.

Tom Jones was up on the porch before he knew what had happened. He just caught a glimpse of the tip of the gray cat's tail flying round the next-door fence. Now that it was all over, he felt a bit shaken, it must be confessed.

"Poor pussin," said Brusque Voice, quite anxiously. "Oh, you're so wet—and bloody—" she said, disappearing into the house and coming back with a clean warm towel with which she rubbed him very gently. And after a while Tom Jones lay down, quite exhausted, under a canvas bed the housekeepers had put on the porch. He could feel the sun through it, and there he laid his torn mouth on one paw and closed his eyes. He ached all over, but that did not prevent a purr of triumph from bubbling up in his chest and throat, of triumph and also of gratitude. For it was rather wonderful to have someone coming and going with saucers of warm milk, and a gentle so-

licitous manner. One does need a
housekeeper on these occasions, he
thought, and then fell asleep, his nose
and paws still twitching now and then.

CHAPTER VII

Tom Jones Keeps
Everything Under Control

WHEN Gentle Voice came home, he was still lying under the canvas bed, for the fact was that he was feeling rather ill.

"Oh dear," she said, "how awful! I expect he will get into one fight after another. And look at his poor mouth— he'll never be the same again."

This was not a very encouraging way to speak, after all, and Tom Jones kept his eyes closed with shame.

"We could take him to the hospital; they might stitch up his wound," Brusque Voice was saying.

"It's that cat next door, that Nelly,"

Gentle Voice said. "She's the trouble-maker. Every Tom for miles around will be after her, and Tom Jones will have to fight them all."

They seemed very much upset. It was, he decided, hard on two such tenderhearted old maids to take in Terrible Jones. But what could he do? Even dignified Mr. Jones must become Terrible Jones when a guttersnipe came and put his nose within two inches of that dignified face and whiffled at it.

He lay on the porch for two days, considering all this, and accepting some special convalescent meals, a plate of the best tuna fish, and some scraps of roast beef, warmed over with gravy. He was very thirsty, too, and drank several saucers of warm milk. Finally after two days and nights, he felt well enough to get up and jump through the window and look around for a soft place to get well in. It was there, lying on a cashmere shawl at the foot of one of the beds, that he realized that he was still the subject of serious concern on the part of his housekeepers. Perhaps because he was feeling rather seedy, the Fur Person was unusually aware of his housekeepers; he had an idea that they were up to mischief, were concealing something from him. They were really rather too attentive, even taking into account that they were two old maids who had obviously been in need of having a Gentleman Cat as lodger for a long time. But they did use the word "hospital" rather a lot considering that he was beginning to feel quite fit and his lower lip had sewn itself together without any help at all, and they allowed him to sleep on the cashmere shawl, clearly a luxury, though one to which he had now become accustomed.

Like any self-respecting cat, Tom Jones took not the slightest interest in other people's affairs unless he was himself concerned in them. So he had hardly paid sufficient attention to the foibles and follies of these two odd and endearing creatures who had taken him in. Now he found himself sometimes considering them when he really should have been doing his yoga exercises, sitting on the cashmere shawl with his paws tucked in and his tail wound round him very carefully, so the white tip (there were certain advantages to such a very long tail) stood straight up beside the curve of his back leg.

What were they really like? he asked himself. The one he liked best was Gentle Voice because it was her voice which had first caught his ear and it was her way of caressing him which had made it plain that he had found a home and the proper care. She disappeared every day for a very long time and came home tired, and while she was away the other housekeeper was sometimes quite absent-minded and even forgot his lunch once or twice because she sat for hours and hours in front of a typewriter, tapping out messages with her fingers—but to whom these messages were addressed he could not figure out. Sometimes when he was feeling friendly he came and sat on the desk and watched her fingers for a while, and had a little talk about what might be for lunch. But sometimes she was talking to herself about something and he would sit down beside her chair and do his yoga exercises and be quite happy just because they were not trying to communicate. In fact he liked her best when she stayed quiet for hours

at a time and he could come and go as
he pleased.

And of course he was very busy keeping everything under control in the
household. After breakfast he had to
read the newspaper. This meant going
way down the hall to the parlor, a room
he avoided at all other times. However,
at about nine each morning when Gentle Voice was ready to go out, he
climbed up in the front window and
sat on a pile of books and found out
what was happening in the world.
From here he could note which dogs
had gone for their morning walks and
were safely out of the way, and whether
any half-friends or enemies among the
cats in the neighborhood were likely to
be about. This sometimes meant reading the newspaper for an hour or more.
By then he had digested his breakfast
and was ready to begin the serious business of his morning toilette. There
seemed to be a great deal of soot about
in this neighborhood and it was quite
a problem to keep his paws, his shirt
front, and the white tip of his tail clean,
as well as the soft teddy-bearish brown
fur on his stomach of which he was so
proud. Then he must lick down each

broad black stripe on his back, and, finally, though his tongue was often quite tired, he must clean his whiskers, get the sleep out of his eyes, and especially rub very hard behind his ears. About then he usually felt the need of a midmorning snack; sometimes there was a little leftover breakfast which might just do. But sometimes not. Then he came very softly into Brusque Voice's room and stared at her back until she was mesmerized into turning around, and even (when she had written a great many messages and needed a morning snack herself) perhaps letting him escort her to the kitchen and see what might be around for elevenses: a small piece of cake crumbled up, or even a dry biscuit would do very well.

By now Tom Jones was quite exhausted with his morning's business and generally decided that it was time for a snooze. It was then, just before he curled a paw round his nose, that he considered his housekeepers and wondered what they might be plotting. They seemed to have only one serious fault and that was the need to break up his fights with pails of water. It was a method which lacked dignity. Even more, Mr. Jones now suspected that they were determined in some way to curtail his activities out of doors, and his need to become a respected member of the community. They did not perhaps realize how important it was at this stage, when he was moving in on a rigid hierarchy, that he establish himself through many a tense and fearful battle.

"He's a tom," Gentle Voice would say, as if this were not the best thing in the world to be. "There's no getting around it." After all, she had named him Tom Jones herself, so whatever was she talking about? Why hadn't she named him Sam Jones, or Timothy Jones if that was the way she felt about it? Were they contemplating giving him a new name?

It never occurred to the Fur Person that what they were contemplating was to change his personality, not his name, to change *him*, in fact, into a believer in non-violence, a Quaker cat for whom the glories of doing battle and tearing out the fur of enemies would become anathema. This was the meaning of the word "altered" which, with the word "hospital," haunted their conversation. And Tom Jones knew these must be dangerous words because they always looked at him so commiseratingly when they used them, and gave him extra pieces of roast beef, as if they had told him a lie and were feeling rather guilty about it.

CHAPTER VIII

Poor Jones Has
a Hard Time

HE HAD suspected that something was brewing but The Thing Itself took him wholly by surprise. In the first place he was thrust into a pillowcase with a string tied round it, at his neck, so only his head emerged and he was a Gentleman Cat made into a peculiar kind of struggling baby. His first instinct, of course, was to escape (the eighth Commandment of the Gentleman Cat is: "Never allow constraint of your person under any circumstances."). But he was after all quite mature and he soon realized that struggle would achieve nothing. So he quieted down, his eyes very big and alarmed, and was carried out into the automobile which Brusque Voice was always driving off in and which made hideous noises and a disagreeable smell. He had often watched this happen from behind the snowball bush. Now he was himself sitting in Gentle Voice's lap in the front seat of the car, all tied up in a pillowcase, and they were flying off at an alarming speed. Very soon, he could no longer recognize a single tree or house and at this point he became so anxious that he could not restrain his mews and began a series of protestations and miaowing in many keys, not once but over and over. It was the worst experience he had ever had, bar none. It was worse than being imprisoned in the stuffy apartment with that suffocating woman, because at least then he had been in control. It was worse than being an orphan with no name; it was worse than finding the perfect garden, house and old lady only to discover that another cat was already in residence. For now he was in such a state of anxiety that he could do nothing but howl, throwing the whole Ten Command-

ments of the Gentleman Cat to the
winds, forgetting all about dignity and
not showing your feelings, because he
was in a real panic. He hardly heard
the two Voices' gentle comforting
words, and after all, what were words
when they had humiliated him by making him into a baby in a pillowcase
and were taking him God knows
where? He could not concentrate at all
on what they said, and did not even
try. He just howled.

Fortunately the Fur Person, like any
respectable animal, had unlimited
amounts of patience to draw on, and
what he did in the hospital was simply
to wait for the strange experience to be
over, a prolonged and exhausting yoga
exercise which left him quite weak, so
weak that he hardly responded when
at long last Gentle Voice lifted him out
of his cage, and he knew that he had
been rescued. Every now and then on
the way home in the car he said a few
words, a few loud complaining words
about what had happened to him, but
he was quite unable to purr, had perhaps forgotten how—he lay there, his
mouth slightly open, panting, until finally Brusque Voice swung the car into

his own street, opened the door, and he was (Oh bliss! Oh, unutterable bliss!) *free.* He staggered a bit, for he had been cooped up in a very small cage, then he raised his nose in ecstasy to sniff the fresh air, the sweet outdoor spring air smelling of earth, and grass and daffodils and rain. Very gently and tentatively his tail rose from a horizontal to a vertical position and he was just about to make a wild joyful dash down the street when he was seized by a coughing fit. No, it would be wiser for the present to go in and lie down.

"His face has grown quite pointed," said Gentle Voice in a grieving tone. "Poor Tom, poor puss . . ." she murmured, stroking him down the long black line on his back. He followed her from room to room until she realized that what he needed was a lap, and at long last, for the Fur Person had become quite desperate holding back the purrs, agreed to settle in the little armchair in the dining room. There he curled himself up on the good warm lap and kneaded a little very gently, and sang a home-coming song, but it was so faint and exhausted a song that he himself could hardly remember it afterwards.

"I don't like that cough," Brusque Voice said the next morning. It was quite true that whenever Tom Jones had a really good idea like running up the pear tree in the back yard, or digging an especially good hole, he was seized by this irritating cough and thoroughly shaken.

"He's not feeling at all well," Gentle Voice answered. "Oh dear—that awful hospital . . ." and Tom Jones gave a faint tremble and felt the need of lying down, because the word "hospital" had become such a strange frightening word. The fact was that whatever they might think, he knew that he was not himself. He could barely remember what it had been like to be Terrible Jones and tear pieces of fur out of nameless enemies. His eyes never did seem to get clean though he washed and washed them until his paw and tongue were quite worn out. Worse, pretty soon he realized that the itching on his head was not just ordinary "time-for-a-lick-and-a-nibble" itching, but something far worse. When he nibbled himself hard, pieces of his own fur came out in his mouth. And after a few days, there were furless places on top of his head and round his ears.

When a cat begins to lose his fur, it is a very humiliating and terrible thing. Tom Jones sat with his paws tucked in on the floor and did not even feel like reading the newspaper. He who had been so full of self-respect that his walk (his tail vertical, his paws lifted lightly and gracefully) was a delight to behold, now felt an impulse to hide and walked very slowly with his tail floating out behind him in a melancholy and unself-respecting way. He looked and felt so forlorn that he lost all appetite. And about this time it occurred to him that his housekeepers might give notice, that if he became a permanent invalid, they would no longer care to look after him. He knew how much they enjoyed stroking the top of his head and now there was nothing to stroke. And how often had he heard them exclaiming about his large green eyes, which grew marvelously dark at night and marvelously pale in the morning. Now they looked at him and said humiliating things like,

"Poor puss, he does look a sight, I must confess."

And one day Brusque Voice said, "Nobody could love him who had not known him before. But we love him, don't we? And we won't abandon him."

It was she who brought a disgusting bottle of greasy stuff with a hospital smell and rubbed it into his fur twice a day. Tom Jones was by now beyond caring and had gone into a depression so deep, that he allowed her to do this, from sheer inertia. His purring machine even creaked a good deal and it hurt him to purr because it reminded him of the days when his purrs were sheer poetry and he himself a swaggering, handsome Gentleman Cat with a white tip to his tail. Ah, he thought, taking a surreptitious look, after all I still do have the white tip to my tail. And I must not despair.

When he went out for his daily walk, he had to bear the insults of any cat who happened to be passing by, and when he heard a song of battle in the distance he ran home as fast as he could. He did not have the strength or the will to fight. Only a strange thing was happening little by little. He was coming to understand that even if he never got well at all, his housekeepers were now more than housekeepers, they were true friends and they would not abandon him. He was really and truly safe. They did not love him for his glossy tiger coat, nor for his white shirt front and white paws, nor for his great green eyes, no, not even for the white tip to his tail. They loved him because he was himself.

feeling to understand that even if he
never got well at all, his housekeeper
were now more than housekeepers
...up to me them...
...went out other...
(made for her...
the...and see...
...he...
between...
...

CHAPTER IX

Glorious Jones or
The Catnip Hangover

As SOON as he had come to understand that he was loved for himself, he
began to feel a little better. One day
he licked his paws as white as snow,
and one day he realized that a thin
new crop of fur was growing in the
bare patches on the top of his head. After that it seemed only a little while
before he was himself again: his coat
grew thick and glossy, his shirt front
shone as brilliant white as ever, and the
white tip of his tail was often carried
like a flag as he walked. Best of all, the
cough entirely disappeared and he
knew he was worthy of being ad-

dressed as Mr. Jones and respectfully saluted by fur people or anyone at all he happened to meet when taking his morning walk.

He was almost his old self, but not quite, for he was never to be Terrible Jones again. Somehow or other whatever had happened at the hospital had changed his nature and he was now a Gentle Cat rather than a Gentleman Cat. His philosophy of life had become mellow and peaceful, and when he was insulted he adopted Passive Resistance (which meant walking slowly away and not coming back to sing rude songs, whatever might be said to him of an insulting kind by less evolved members of the community). The idea of a fight made him feel sad, and a little anxious. He had become a Cat of Peace.

All this meant that he was out of doors rambling and roving much less than he used to be and it was necessary that he invent some indoor activities to keep himself busy and fit. In this the housekeepers were most understanding. One day Gentle Voice came home and the Fur Person, who was sitting on the porch with his paws tucked in, taking the evening air, ran out to meet her. She showed him her big bag of books and papers as if he should be interested in it, for some reason. And, quite true, Dear me, he thought, what a very strange and attractive smell it has. So he followed her indoors, filled with curiosity, and wound himself around her legs, purring the purr of ardent desire like a kettle coming to a boil and then bubbling very fast.

"Come here," she called to the other housekeeper, and spread out a newspaper. "I have some catnip for Tom Jones."

The Fur Person had forgotten all about the third commandment which concerns approach to food and how a Gentleman Cat must never look eager. He stood up on tiptoe and tried to get his head into the bag, he was so excited by this wonderful, intoxicating smell. Then he scratched a few times with his paw to inform the housekeepers that he was getting impatient and that they (not young, poor dears) were being very slow indeed about satisfying his need to examine whatever it was that had the smell, and to do it without further delay. But finally the newspaper

was spread and Gentle Voice took out
a little bundle of soft green leaves and
laid them down. It was such a powerful
smell that the Fur Person for a second
hesitated to go near it; he crouched
down, his cinnamon nose trembling, his
eyes narrowed as if the flat bundle of
dead leaves were a mouse and he
would like to pounce on it and tear it
to pieces. But before he could make up
his mind, he was so attracted that he
could not stop to consider and with one
swoop of his paw gathered up the
leaves and chewed them frantically, as
if he were starving and this green stuff
were the very best of meat.

"He likes it very much," Brusque
Voice said. The housekeepers beamed
at each other because they were delighted when they could do anything
to please a cat who had been so ill and
now was well.

Tom Jones paused and ran his
tongue over his chops a few times to
get the last lingering taste, so aromatic,
so unlike any food he had ever tasted
before. While he licked his chops he realized that he felt a little dizzy and at
the same time elated, and quite suddenly he knew that what was required

now was to lie down on his back and roll and roll on what was left of the catnip.

"Oh look, he's rolling," Gentle Voice said and in the middle of his roll, all four feet in the air and the whole of his soft teddy-bear tummy exposed, he opened starfish paws and looked up languorously at these wonderful house-keepers who knew just what he needed. He rolled all the way over to one side and lay there, then he rolled back, then he rolled himself to a sitting position and took one more tiny taste of the cat-nip. Then he knew that he was just too full of something to keep still and he raced down the hall and back again, leaped up on the bed and stood there, waving his tail, his eyes blazing. And for the first time in weeks he began to compose a very loud happy song all about himself and how wonderful he was:

> I'm a whiffling wonder
> And my purr's like thunder,
> I'm an elegant fellow
> And my temper's mellow
> And my eyes as green
> As have ever been seen;

I've a coat like silk
Paws white as milk,
I'm a catly cat,
An aristocrat.
If you wish to see
Tom Jones, I'm he,
This Jones victorious
Glossy and glorious,
Lordly and lazy
And catnip crazy,
Yes, glorious Jones
    Is me!

"Goodness," said Gentle Voice, "he does look pleased with himself!" "He's simply roaring," said Brusque Voice, "and look, he's making starfish paws in the air, how sweet!"

For Glorious Jones, as he now knew himself to be, had just discovered that it was a very delightful thing to knead the air just as if all that surrounded him, the whole world, were a gigantic lap. He lifted one paw and spread it out and in, and his eyes grew soft. Then he lifted the other and tried the same thing, and his eyes grew softer. In fact he was feeling extremely sentimental by now.

Dear me, he thought, do you suppose

I have had too much catnip and shall always be like this, dizzy with love and self-adulation? But just then he keeled over and found himself stretched out on the bed, almost asleep.

"He'll sleep it off," said Brusque Voice, tickling him behind one ear. "It's a catnip hangover."

So they tiptoed away and left him, and pretty soon his purrs grew quite faint, until there were long pauses between each one, and finally he gave a tremulous sigh, his back foot twitched once, and then he lay perfectly still.

CHAPTER X

The Mouse Is at Large!

AFTER that there were occasional green-letter Catnip Days, and there were also splendid Mouse-catching Days. Now that Terrible Jones was Glorious Jones, and more often just plain Gentle Jones, he did not find hunting as amusing as it had once been. He still occasionally went to the window and chattered at a passing bird, but this was more because he liked to hear his teeth clicking than anything else. He did not feel that he had to catch the bird. He preferred to observe life in general rather than to pounce upon it. As for mice, there had never been any around to catch, even when he was Terrible Jones, but he did sometimes think that a nice playful mouse would make for a pleasant change. After all, one could not read the newspaper all day long, even when one had become a Cat of Peace.

The housekeepers who had his comfort and happiness so much at heart, took this all into consideration and one day Brusque Voice came home from an expedition with a little paper bag in her hand. She came and rattled the bag softly at the Fur Person, who for some reason, had been feeling a bit low in his mind. Or perhaps simply a trifle bored. He had read and reread the newspaper; he had done a little desultory beehunting in the garden, but a dreadful old black guttercat had come and stared at him with such contempt that he came home and did yoga exercises for quite a while just to get over the humiliation. Now he pricked up his ears and turned his head sideways to have a look. Catnip, he asked himself? No, he answered himself, as his nose trembled at the bag, but got no sensation at all, except the bland pasty smell of paper itself. Whatever could it be?

"It's a mouse," Gentle Voice said, for she came in just then to find out what was up.

And indeed Brusque Voice had now opened the bag right near his nose and laid before him a soft gray mouse with a long elastic tail, real whiskers, two very bright eyes and pale pink ears, and even (for now she turned it over) tiny pale pink feet underneath its fat woolly body.

The Fur Person was not amused. A toy mouse for me? he thought, standing up to his full height on tiptoe and arching his back, then giving a tremendous yawn. A toy mouse for a catly cat, for a dignified cat like me?

But the toy mouse had such bright eyes that for just a second Tom Jones thought it winked at him. He put out a soft paw and touched it tentatively. The tail trembled in a rather inviting way and he batted it off the bed with one masterly swing of his paw. And— Tom Jones could have sworn this—it actually bounded off, ran away and hid under the radiator. This was really more like it. The Fur Person crouched on the bed, his whiskers bristling and held well forward, his cinnamon nose

trembling slightly, his eyes fixed on the
mouse though not a muscle of his body
moved. He could feel small electric cur-
rents running up and down his spine,
and then, as the pupils of his eyes
opened wide with the excitement of not
pouncing, his hindquarters began to
shiver and shake and his tail to lash
back and forth, and suddenly he was in
the air. His tail lifted in a great arc as
he landed, and with one furious exact
swat of a paw he sent the mouse scurry-
ing right across the room. This time he
leaped after it without even waiting to
see where it would land. He ran to it,
joyfully, and began to bat it along the
floor, first with one paw then with the
other, in a swift glide like a hockey
player with a puck. Then he did a sideways dance, his four paws very close
together, his back arched, and then
suddenly leapt into the air, caught the
mouse between his teeth as he landed,
and carried it out into the hall.

There he laid it down and sat for a
while, catching his breath, and pretending that he had forgotten all about
it. Once he looked at it out of the corner of an eye, found it irresistible and
threw it high into the air, caught it

with one paw, threw it again and began the hockey game once more, bat and glide, glide and bat, all down the hall.

His housekeepers applauded all this and he felt very gay and good and beautiful indeed. For now that he had changed into Gentle Jones, now that he would not fight, now that he had accepted that the housekeepers were faithful whatever happened, and even if he lost his fur, he felt the need of human admiration more than ever before. In fact he had not needed it at all when he was a Gentleman Cat About Town. But he did now feel the need of being told how handsome he was, to be applauded and praised. And because of this he was ready to give the housekeepers a little more of his real cat self than he had ever yielded to anyone or anything before. When they went out, he sometimes spent hours not even doing his yoga exercises, just waiting for them to come home, because the house did not feel quite like home if they were absent. And sometimes he made up little songs about this to console himself, because the house was so very silent:

When you go away
I forget how to play.
When you're not there
I forget how to purr.
Your voice in the house
Means "food," means "mouse,"
And your kind lap
Is my warm soft sleep.
I make starfish paws
For your applause,
And I had no name
Until you came
So for all these things
Jones sits and sings
And for all these ways
Tom is filled with praise.

Of course there were times when perfect peace did not reign in this well-run
loving household. For instance Tom
sometimes got bored with his mouse
and left it way under the daybed in the
parlor, or hidden behind a radiator and
then the next day couldn't be bothered
to find it. So when the housekeepers
came home, eager to play, the mouse
was not to be found.

"The mouse is at large," Gentle Voice
would cry out, as if the mouse were
some Very Large Terrible Tiger who

might leap out upon them from behind a door. Then the Fur Person watched them with a faintly cynical expression in his tender green eyes, while they got down on their hands and knees and searched under beds and under chairs and under radiators—and sometimes it was days and days before the elusive mouse turned up. But after all, Tom Jones had now and then to show his independence. He had to keep his dignity, even if he had given such a large part of his life into human keeping—or perhaps just because he had done so, he must not lose his dignity. So, every now and then, he went on a rove and a ramble all by himself, and stayed away for hours, climbing a tree or two, or exploring a back yard several streets away, or paying a brief call at one or other of the grocers' in the neighborhood, just in case a small piece of raw liver might be about. Besides he had to keep a census of the local cats, and to know what was going on, even though he chose to have no part in the ludicrous wars for position and power which ungentle, terrible cats kept up for appearance's sake. Then for a few hours at a time he forgot about his ob-

ligations and responsibilities at home
and became a catly cat again. It was a
great relief to dash up a tree and down
again, with no one at all to watch or
applaud. It was a great relief to be a
cat and nothing but a cat, and to be
busy with his own affairs. However, after a long ramble and several small ad-
ventures—such as coming face to face
with a huge barking black dog, making
a very fat tail and spitting until the dog
was routed—after all this he would begin to feel a queer tug in his breast, a
tug which said, "Home, Jones," a tug
which made him feel rather tight inside
and just a little anxious. "How are
they?" the tug said, and his heart began to beat rather fast. And sometimes
he was forced to run the whole way
back because the tug became so strong
and he was suddenly afraid that he
had missed Something.

One day when this happened and he
bounded up onto the porch and, forgetting all about the Commandment
about never mewing, actually climbed
up to the window and gave a loud cry
to say "I'm home again. Where are
you?", nobody came. They had gone
out. His heart was beating so fast in

panic that he had to sit down at once and tuck his paws in and do his yoga exercises with immense concentration, to keep out the woe which was growing inside him like a balloon. The exercises helped a little, but he could not get rid entirely of the woe.

His ears were pricked for every step along the brick pavement. He had learned long ago to listen for the click-click of Gentle Voice's feet along the walk and for Brusque Voice's longer stride. The balloon of anxiety was growing so big that he got up and walked up and down, his tail laid out on the air straight behind him in a way that suggested pure melancholy.

And when they did come home at last, not on foot, but roaring up in the car and slamming the doors, he ran as fast as he could and rubbed against their legs and purred and purred, so they were quite astonished.

"He must be starving," Gentle Voice said. "He's been out for hours."

But he could not explain that it was not hunger this time that made him tremble with joy and go round and round looking up into their dear human faces, but only that he was so very hap-

py that they had come home at last,
and that he had missed them very
much. It was really hardly worth going
off on a ramble when it made him so
anxious, and he decided there and then
to stay near by. There must be other
ways to maintain his dignity. There
must be less costly ways.

CHAPTER XI

The Great Move

THE Fur Person was now so thoroughly settled and at home that sheer peace of mind made him grow quite fat, and no one ever stopped to say "Poor Puss," any more, but instead they admired his glossy coat and actually called him "A HUGE CAT." The question of maintaining his dignity and yet staying at home was solved by sheer bulk. It was not a matter of making expeditions at all. It was a matter of being the Lord of the House and keeping a firm paw on the housekeepers, exerting his will now and then by refusing to eat unless they remembered that he required the first quality stew beef and only the very best fresh haddock: as long as it was quite clear in everyone's mind who was Master, the question of dignity did not occur. He was even able to accept that the housekeepers did need an occasional holiday and when this happened must delegate a substitute to see that the Fur Person was well looked after in their absence. So it happened that over the years a young man spent part of the summer at the house and the housekeepers went away. The Fur Person rather enjoyed making the acquaintance of this gentle young man, came and went on his business as usual, read his newspaper, and was altogether patient and polite, for he knew that sooner or later the housekeepers would come back and all be as before.

But wise and fat though he had grown, the Fur Person had never imagined the possibility that his housekeepers might be asked to move away, that they would no longer be able to walk down to the end of the garden with him and look at the pear tree, or kneel in the flower plot with baskets of pansies and forget-me-nots beside them, that they would in fact be forcibly uprooted from this ideal house and garden and have to find another place to live. Yet this is just what did happen; it happened when Brusque Voice was away and Gentle Voice all alone to search and find, to pack and go, to tie up bundles, to roll up blankets, to take down hundreds of books from the bookcases while the Fur Person watched her with his green eyes very wide open and his tail a question mark trembling in the air. For some time he thought perhaps Gentle Voice was in a fury of summer cleaning and that everything would be unpacked again pretty soon: in that case he would go out and lie under a lilac bush until it was all over. But when he saw that an enormous van had come to the door and some terrible men with loud voices were actually carrying his own bed into it, as well as the big armchair and the couch from the study, so that literally he would have nowhere to lay his head, the Fur Person became very much alarmed.

He crept away and hid under the window seat in the parlor, no question now of reading the newspaper. It was

a moment of terrible decision. If only
he knew *where* they were going! In
order to compose his mind he licked
both back paws for a long long time
and gave his ears and whiskers a thorough going over, and all the time he
was trying to remember a commandment which had grown rather dim
through these years of comfort.
It seemed to go something like this: "A
Gentleman Cat Attaches Himself to
Places Rather Than to People." He
brought his whiskers forward and
looked judiciously at them down his
nose. He had never questioned a commandment before in his life, for the
commandments were not something he
made up all by himself like his songs:
they welled up inside him and con-
tained the wisdom of generations of
Gentlemen Cats. When in doubt, remember the Commandments, had until now seemed a safe solution to almost
any problem. Stay here and let the
housekeepers go on their way without
him? His whiskers trembled a little and
his green eyes became thin hard slits.

After all, it was not to be supposed
that ever again would he find himself
in a house with such a perfect pear tree

to climb in, or such lovely round posts for sharpening his claws, or that wherever the housekeepers went there would be such a convenient safe porch where he could sit in the sun. But then he remembered the laps, where he had lain so cozily for so many years, being caressed with such great *savoir-faire;* and he remembered that first dish of warm haddock, so fresh and white and altogether delicious, and the catnip hangover and the playful mouse. And he remembered the time when his fur came out and he was so very ill and the housekeepers had served him faithfully and never complained. That was too much. He crept out from under the window seat and walked through the empty rooms, his tail held high, looking for Gentle Voice.

He purred, winding himself round her legs, and this meant I am going where you go. Of course she had no idea that he had decided to break one of the commandments nor what heart-searching had just been going on under the window seat. She was very busy carrying armloads of coats out to the van, and she hardly paid any attention at all.

It was clear that if he did not do
something right away he would begin
to feel terribly lonely and sad, now he
was sitting in the middle of an empty
bedroom with nowhere at all to lay his
head. So he sat upright and hummed
a rather long and ragged self-justifying
song to himself and the world at large:

If you break the law
You'll have itching paw
And anxieties
Will behave like fleas
Biting here or there
But you can't find where;
All of this I sense
From experience,
But for all of that
I'm a free wise cat
True philosopher
And I'll make my purr
And I'll take my stand
With humankind,
Paw in your hand,
Mine to command,
I won't let you go.
I am coming too.

Perhaps he would not have had the
courage to make up such a brave song

if he could have foreseen how he would spend the greater part of that terrible day, nor what humiliations lay in store for a Gentleman Cat who had broken the commandment about places rather than people. For the time came when there was nothing left in the house at all, except some piles of rubbish and Tom Jones, and after that the even worse time came when he was picked up by Gentle Voice and thrust into a taxi with her and rushed off through strange streets with not a moment in which to prepare himself for the Great Change, and not even a saucer of milk in his gullet, so his desperate miaow came out thin and scratchy, and it occurred to him that he was actually losing his voice!

And as if all this treatment, so offensive to his dignity and trust, were not enough, he was ignominiously thrust into a cold dank garage, which smelled of gasoline and peat moss and old dirty rags and lumber, and the doors were locked. There was no window he could reach, so he could not even discover where he was. The need to explore, to orient himself by nose, paw and eye, was completely frustrated, and he suddenly became furiously angry, more angry than he had ever been in his life. He lashed his tail and paced up and down this prison, shouting his rage and despair at the walls and hearing his words echo back at him. No one came. No one paid the slightest attention or seemed aware that the Lord of the new house was a prisoner. He was so terribly angry that all he could do was swear; he could not even turn the swears into a song, which might have given him some satisfaction. He was so terribly angry that he stepped right into a pool of grease and got his white paws coal black and disgusting. He was so angry by then that he did not feel he could stop to clean up—that would have been to appear to be resigned. He was so angry that he felt he was twice his normal size, and he prepared to leap at anyone who opened the door and give them a piece of his mind in no uncertain terms. His voice grew hoarse with so much unaccustomed screaming and yelling, but still he kept on, and even took a couple of running jumps at the big garage doors and banged himself against them.

It was dark by the time Gentle Voice

came to let him out. He had been sitting with his nose pressed to the crack, too tired to speak, in a state of despair. But as soon as the door opened, he became a ball of lightning and flew out without a word, not knowing where he was bound except to get away, to climb a tree, to assert himself as a free animal again. And, oh, the air was sweet, and the maple by the door, as he raced past, inviting!

> This is my tree
> And you won't catch me

he sang hurriedly as he sprang into the air, caught the trunk in a furious embrace and ran up it so fast, he thought himself he might suddenly have learned to fly. Then, way up on nearly the topmost branch, he stood up and glared around him, and looked down with hard black eyes at Gentle Voice, a tiny feeble human being standing by the trunk, saying how sorry she was and begging him to come down right away, and she would give him some supper.

For answer he lashed his tail three times and bounded to an even more perilous branch, which swayed under his weight so that he almost lost his balance.

He did not come in for a long time. After all, it was now or never; it was absolutely necessary that it be made clear, once and for all, who was master. He had chosen to come with Gentle Voice to the new house of his own free will, and then he had been treated like a foolish kitten who might run away and get lost and who would not know the law about complete exploration of every nook and cranny of a new neighborhood. So off he went, down the street, the strange street, mighty in his anger, ready to growl and pounce on anyone who might try to stop him. He swaggered the whole length of the street and discovered a huge playground with almost an acre of long grass, trees and wildness to wander in just around the corner. From there he could hear Gentle Voice calling anxiously in the dark,

"Here puss, here puss—please come home!"

Had she been punished enough? No, but he was rather too hungry, and a Gentleman Cat always sees that his own needs come first. So at long last, he stood at the open door and allowed himself to be caressed and cajoled and led through the house to the kitchen where Gentle Voice laid before him, very humbly, a large dish of fresh white steaming haddock, as a peace offering.

Much later on when he was lying on her bed, with his paws tucked in, looking at her in rather a sentimental way and purring very softly, she told him, "This is our house, you know, and we shall never have to move again."

CHAPTER XII

The Eleventh Commandment
or the Reflections of a
Window-box Cat

THE next morning bright and early, while Gentle Voice was still fast asleep, Tom Jones made a thorough exploration of the house (after all it is something to be presented with a house even if you are a very distinguished Gentle Cat) and was well satisfied with all that he found. There was, in the first place, a quite magnificent cellar with several different rooms in it, a delightful coalbin, a woodpile, and just the right musty earthy smell. Best of all, a quite perfect newspaper-reading place had been arranged on the corner of the piano, in the parlor. Yes, it really would do very well, thought the Fur Person,

sitting upright, feeling dignified indeed
as he considered the morning news.

There seemed to be a great many
cats in this neighborhood, a fact which
he noted with some alarm. Some had
collars and bells; one had rather a sinister black and white face and sneered
up at the window as he went past. But
at least they were not ruffians; they
were all catly cats with homes and
names, and no doubt they would pay a
neighborly call and he could then inform them that he was a Cat of Peace
and did not intend to fight for position
in the community. Still, when Gentle
Voice came down at last and opened
the door to let him out into the warm
summer air, he did feel a slight prickling in his spine; he did hope he found
himself in a genteel neighborhood
where his convictions would be respected. And just to give himself confidence he sang a gentle song to the
world at large:

> I have come disarmed.
> I have come for good
> Among you, my friends;
> I am greatly charmed
> By this neighborhood

Where my story ends,
So be gentle, do
And accept my state
For I will not fight
Whatever you do,
I'm a gentle cat
And it is my right
To sit in the sun
On this lovely street
On a fine June morning
And to anyone
I may chance to meet
I give this warning:
I'm a Gentle Cat
And I will not FIGHT.

Almost at once a beautiful fat fluffy
cat with a bell on its neck ran across
and gave Tom Jones a friendly greeting, nose to nose. And just to show his
gratitude Tom Jones ran halfway up
the convenient maple just by the door,
and down again. Pretty soon the black
and white fluffy cat was joined by a
gray kitten, who lay down and rolled
over and asked the Fur Person to play
in such a confiding and seductive way
that he forgot all about dignity and
chased it for quite some moments, and
felt himself becoming a kind of jocular

Uncle who would indulge an adopted nephew with many a tender mock battle. But all of a sudden the kitten made a huge tail and began to say some terrible words and Tom Jones turned round like lightning, just in time to meet the sinister black and white face he had observed from the window, leering at him.

Well, it was a rather tense moment. No time really to explain about being a Cat of Peace, or to sing his song. Instead he gave a wild look around and could hardly believe his eyes when he saw that just by the door of his own house, just under the newspaper window, a convenient window box, apparently designed for this very purpose, invited him to take refuge. With hardly a look behind him he had jumped up the three cement steps and found himself rather like a sailor in a boat, rather like a lighthouse keeper in a lighthouse, rather like a bird in a nest, rather like a flowerpot in a window box quite safely ensconced and looking down in a lordly way at the sinister cat, sitting below.

"I wish it to be quite clear," snarled the sinister cat, "that I'm King of the Cats about here, and you will keep your place. If anyone plays with that foolish kitten, I do. If anyone sits in the best patch of sun on any of the porches, I do. These gardens, these houses, this street, and all these cats are subject to me," growled the sinister cat, lashing his tail in a very menacing way.

The Fur Person sat straight up in his Window Box and looked down rather like an Admiral of the Fleet, rather like a Lighthouse Keeper, rather like a Very Old Wise Owl. He hummed to himself

> I'm a gentle cat
> And I will not fight.

Then when he was perfectly in control of himself, and his whiskers had stopped trembling, he did two yoga exercises. The sinister cat was so astonished by this lack of the usual response that he had to sit down. After several seconds of silence he could not believe his ears when he heard the peculiar new cat say:

"Very well, if you do not wish to be my friend, you may be my semifriend."

The jingling of the fluffy cat's bells sounded like laughter, and the kitten ran up the tree and looked back rather saucily, so the sinister cat did not know where to look nor how to deal with such unexpected forgiveness. He did not even know for sure who had won in this first of many semifriendly skirmishes.

But the Fur Person learned then and there that it is better to be a philosopher than to be a king and that, all things considered, wisdom was to be preferred to power. Sometimes he lay on his back in the window box, one paw languorously resting on its edge and looked up at the leaves and said over to himself The Commandments of the Gentleman Cat, and tried to get them into a proper sequence. For he had learned them in a rather helter-skelter way through all the experiences of his life and now that he had a house of his own and had become an Official Philosopher, it was high time that he put his ideas in order. Perhaps, he thought (on a rather warm afternoon, when he had nothing better to do), they might be arranged like this:

The Ten Commandments of The Gentleman Cat

I. A Gentleman Cat has an immaculate shirt front and paws at all times.

II. A Gentleman Cat allows no constraint of his person, even loving constraint.

III. A Gentleman Cat does not mew except in extremity. He makes his wishes known and waits.

IV. When addressed, a Gentleman Cat does not move a muscle. He looks as if he hadn't heard.

V. When frightened, a Gentleman Cat looks bored.

VI. A Gentleman Cat takes no interest in other people's affairs, unless he is directly concerned.

VII. A Gentleman Cat never hurries toward an objective, never looks as if he wanted just one thing: it is not polite.

VIII. A Gentleman Cat approaches food slowly, however hungry he may be, and decides at least three feet away whether it is Good, Fair, Passable or Unworthy. If Unworthy, he pretends to scratch earth over it.

    IX. A Gentleman Cat gives thanks for a Worthy meal, by licking the plate so clean that a person might think it had been washed.

    X. A Gentleman Cat is never hasty when choosing a housekeeper.

It had been rather hard work remembering all these commandments and putting them in proper order, so the Fur Person withdrew his paw and fell asleep, lying upside down and enjoying the little breeze that ruffled the soft teddy-bear fur on his tummy. He was woken by the voices of his housekeepers, as they came out for a little walk in the soft summer evening. For Brusque Voice had come back now and life was as it always had been.

For some reason the sound of their voices, which had over the years since they had served him, said such tender things, made him prick up his ears, yawn, and then pull himself to his feet and stand on tiptoe arching his back. His eyes grew black with the thought he was thinking, and he began to itch all over, as he always did when he had

a Very Important Idea. After all, he was thinking, as he nibbled a place on his back, and then licked down his shirt front, and finally ran a paw over his ears, for they had begun to itch quite violently—after all, I am not just a Gentleman Cat, I am a far rarer thing, a Gentle Cat, a Cat of Peace, a Cat with a house and two housekeepers, and for me there is perhaps an eleventh Commandment which I should be sure to tell that unlicked kitten of an adopted nephew across the street. It was quite a hard commandment to think out, and to do it the Fur Person sat upright like an Admiral or an Owl for quite a while.

It had to do with dignity; it had to do with reserve; it had to do with freedom—and how these could be maintained when a fur person has given up part of his cat self into human keeping. For the Fur Person might still be the ineffable Mr. Jones walking down the street, greeting man and cat with equal dignity, but he was also an anxious tender personality who followed the two Voices up and down the stairs and round the house, begging for a lap. The Tenth Commandment stated coldly that one had to choose a housekeeper with extreme caution. It said nothing about what happens if and when the housekeeper becomes a true friend, to be trusted in sickness and in health, to be followed from house to house, repaid for the trouble she takes in providing excellent meals with songs and purrs, and in general properly provided with catly attentions. But of course the Eleventh Commandment would have to deal primarily with love —at this point Tom Jones's eyes opened very wide and he stared in front of him with such fixed attention that he did not even notice the semi-friend observing him from behind a tree. His chin began to itch and he washed his face rather thoroughly and scratched his chin with his back foot several times. It is all in the name "Fur Person," he decided then—not really a name at all, but a way of describing the relationship between a Gentle Cat and his true friends among the human people. For a Fur *Person*, he saw in his state of extreme concentration, is not just an ordinary cat. He is a cat who is also a person. And Tom Jones realized that he had called himself the *Fur* Person when he did not really know what a Fur *Person* is. For a Fur *Person* is a cat whom human beings love in the right way, allowing him to keep his dignity, his reserve and his freedom. And a Fur *Person* is a cat who has come to love one or, in very exceptional cases, two human beings, and who had decided to stay with them as long as he lives. This can only happen if the human being has imagined part of himself into a cat (Tom Jones had noticed that Brusque Voice sometimes tried to purr) just as the cat has imagined part of himself into a human being. It is a mutual exchange. A Fur *Person* must be adopted by catly humans, tactful, delicate, respectful, indulgent; these are fairly rare, though not as rare as might be supposed. So thought Tom Jones, and it was the end of such a long think that he was quite exhausted, the Eleventh Commandment must go something like this: A Gentleman Cat becomes a Fur *Person* when he is truly loved by a human being.

It was not exactly a commandment, he realized, but it would have to do, for he was suddenly very sleepy.

SIGNET Books For Your Reference Shelf